Guest Spot

Play-along for Clarinet
CHART TOPPERS

Wise Publications
part of The Music Sales Group
LONDON / NEW YORK / PARIS / SYDNEY / COPENHAGEN / BERLIN / MADRID / HONG KONG / TOKYO

Published by
Wise Publications
14-15 Berners Street, London W1T 3LJ, UK.

Exclusive Distributors:
Music Sales Limited
Distribution Centre, Newmarket Road, Bury St Edmunds,
Suffolk IP33 3YB, UK.
Music Sales Pty Limited
20 Resolution Drive, Caringbah, NSW 2229, Australia

Order No. AM1000340
ISBN 13: 978-1-84938-506-0
This book © Copyright 2010 Wise Publications,
a division of Music Sales Limited.

Engraving, arranging and backing tracks supplied by Camden Music.
Top line arrangements by Chris Hussey.
Backing tracks for The Climb, Cry Me Out, Don't Stop Believin',
Fight For This Love and Love Story programmed by John Maul.
Backing tracks for Bad Romance, Broken Strings and Fireflies
programmed by Danny Gluckstein.

CD recorded, mixed and mastered by Jonas Persson.
Clarinet played by Howard McGill.

Printed in the EU.

Your Guarantee of Quality:
As publishers, we strive to produce every book to
the highest commercial standards.
The music has been freshly engraved and the book has been
carefully designed to minimise awkward page turns and
to make playing from it a real pleasure.
Particular care has been given to specifying acid-free, neutral-sized
paper made from pulps which have not been elemental chlorine bleached.
This pulp is from farmed sustainable forests and was
produced with special regard for the environment.
Throughout, the printing and binding have been planned to
ensure a sturdy, attractive publication which should give years of enjoyment.
If your copy fails to meet our high standards,
please inform us and we will gladly replace it.

www.musicsales.com

Clarinet Fingering Chart

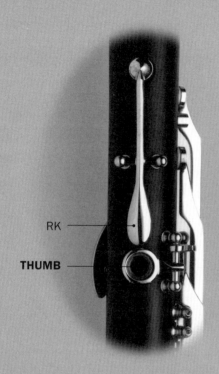

RK

THUMB

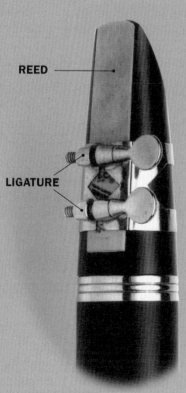

REED

LIGATURE

Mouthpiece

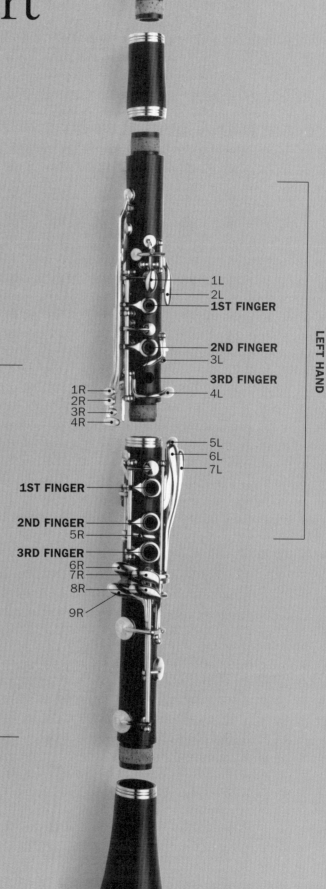

LEFT HAND

1L
2L
1ST FINGER

2ND FINGER
3L

3RD FINGER
4L

1R
2R
3R
4R

5L
6L
7L

1ST FINGER

2ND FINGER
5R

3RD FINGER
6R
7R
8R

9R

RIGHT HAND

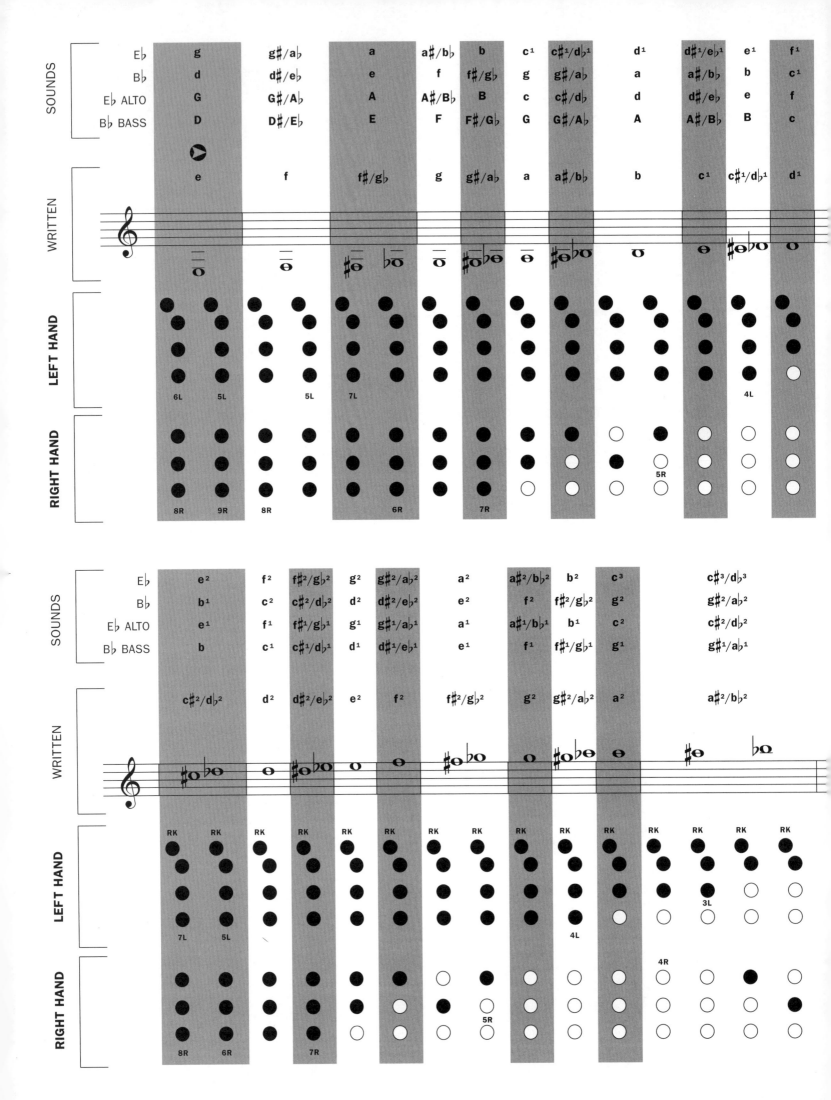

Indicates the lower limit of the best playing range for E♭, B♭, E♭ Alto and B♭ Bass Clarinets

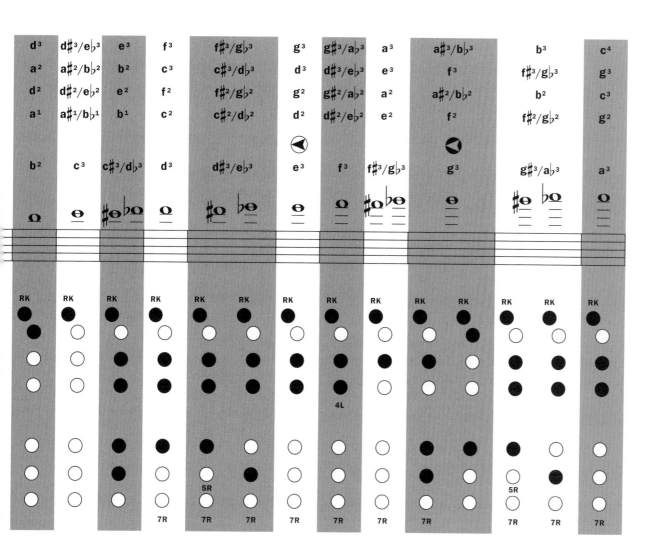

Indicates the upper limit of the best playing range for E♭ and B♭ Clarinets

Indicates the upper limit of the best playing range for E♭ Alto and B♭ Bass Clarinets

Broken Strings (James Morrison/Nelly Furtado)

Words & Music by James Morrison, Fraser T. Smith & Nina Woodford

Bad Romance (Lady Gaga)

Words & Music by Stefani Germanotta & RedOne

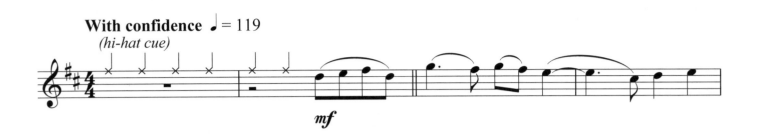

f energico

to Coda

The Climb (Joe McElderry)

Words & Music by Jessica Alexander & Jon Mabe

Cry Me Out (Pixie Lott)

Words & Music by Pixie Lott, Mads Hauge, Phil Thornalley & Colin Campsie

Don't Stop Believin' (Journey)

Words & Music by Steve Perry, Neal Schon & Jonathan Cain

Fireflies (Owl City)

Words & Music by Adam Young

Lightly, with a bounce ♩ = 90

mf leggiero

1° *mp legato*
2° *mf legato*

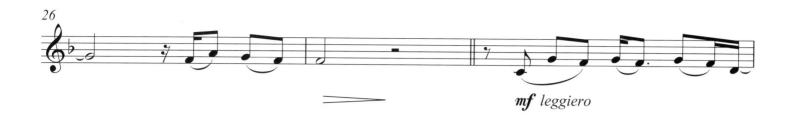

Fight For This Love (Cheryl Cole)

Words & Music by Steve Kipner, Wayne Wilkins & Andre Merritt

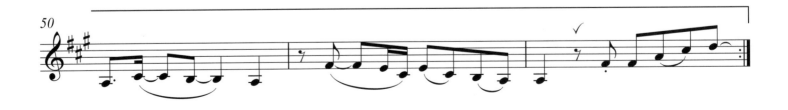

Repeat to fade

Halo (Beyoncé)

Words & Music by Ryan Tedder, Beyoncé Knowles & Evan Bogart

Steadily, with conviction ♩ = 80

(piano cue)

mp

cresc. poco a poco

mf (2°*f*)

D.S. al Coda

Coda

Love Story (Taylor Swift)

Words & Music by Taylor Swift

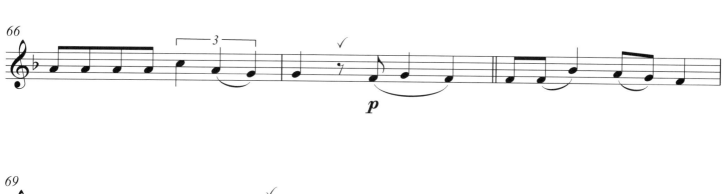

Take A Bow (Rihanna)

Words & Music by Mikkel Eriksen, Tor Erik Hermansen & Shaffer Smith

D.S. al Coda

⊕ **Coda**

molto rit.

2 3 4 5 6 7 8 9

CD Track Listing

Disc 1: Full instrumental performances...

1. Tuning notes

2. Broken Strings
   (Morrison/Smith/Woodford) Chrysalis Music Limited/Sony/ATV Music Publishing

3. Bad Romance
   (Germanotta/RedOne) Sony/ATV Music Publishing (UK) Limited

4. The Climb
   (Alexander/Mabe) Stage Three Music Limited/
   Warner/Chappell Artemis Music Limited

5. Cry Me Out
   (Lott/Hauge/Thornalley/Campsie) Universal Music Publishing MGB Limited/
   Sony/ATV Music Publishing (UK) Limited

6. Don't Stop Believin'
   (Perry/Schon/Cain) IQ Music Limited/Sony ATV Music Publishing (UK) Limited

7. Fireflies
   (Young) Universal/MCA Music Limited.

8. Fight For This Love
   (Kipner/Wilkins/Merritt) Universal Music Publishing Limited/
   EMI Music Publishing Limited/Sony/ATV Music Publishing (UK) Limited/
   Universal/MCA Music Limited

9. Halo
   (Tedder/Knowles/Bogart) Sony/ATV Music Publishing (UK) Limited/
   EMI Music Publishing Limited/Kobalt Music Publishing Limited

10. Love Story
    (Swift) Sony/ATV Music Publishing (UK) Limited

11. Take A Bow
    (Eriksen/Hermansen/Smith) Imagem Music/Sony/ATV Music Publishing (UK) Limited/
    EMI Music Publishing Limited

Disc 2: Backing tracks only...

1. Tuning notes
2. Broken Strings
3. Bad Romance
4. The Climb
5. Cry Me Out
6. Don't Stop Believin'
7. Fireflies
8. Fight For This Love
9. Halo
10. Love Story
11. Take A Bow

To remove your CD from the plastic sleeve,
lift the small lip to break the perforations.
Replace the disc after use for convenient storage